THE THREE BILLY GOATS GRUFF

Dedicated to my loving parents,
Aaron and Teresa
—R. B.

Henry Holt and Company, Inc.
Publishers since 1866
115 West 18th Street
New York, New York 10011

Henry Holt is a registered
trademark of Henry Holt and Company, Inc.

Library of Congress Cataloging-in-Publication Data
Bender, Robert.
The three billy goats Gruff / by Robert Bender.
English retelling of: Asbjørnsen, P.C., Tre bukkene Bruse.
Summary: Three clever billy goats outwit a mean, ugly troll that
lives under the bridge they must cross on their way to a grassy pasture.
[1. Fairy tales.   2. Folklore—Norway.   3. Goats—Folklore.]
I. Asbjørnsen, Peter Christen, 1812-1885.   Tre bukkene Bruse.   II. Title.
PZ8.B42313Th   1993   398.24′5297358—dc20   92-41077

ISBN 0-8050-2529-4

First Edition—1993

Printed in the United States of America on acid-free paper. ∞

1 3 5 7 9 10 8 6 4 2

THE THREE
BILLY GOATS GRUFF

ROBERT BENDER

Henry Holt and Company ◆ New York

Once upon a time, there were three billy goats who all had the name Gruff. They lived very comfortably until . . .

. . . they started running low on the green stuff. They had no choice but to cross over the bridge to eat in the grassy pastures that lay beyond it. Under that bridge, though, lived a mean, ugly troll with foul breath that made the daisies wilt.

First came the littlest billy goat Gruff. *Trip-trap, trip-trap* went the bridge.

"Who's that tripping over my bridge?" grunted the troll.

"It is only I, the puniest billy goat Gruff," the goat said in his meekest voice.

"Good, I'm ready for a tender morsel!" yelled the troll.

"Please don't eat me," cried the little Gruff. "I'm just a low-calorie snack! My bigger brother will be along soon and he'll make a much more satisfying meal."

So the troll rumbled and grumbled, but he let the little goat pass over to the green pastures.

Soon the bridge went *trip-trap, trip-trap* in a louder fashion.

"Who's that tripping over my bridge?" growled the troll.

"It is only I, the middle billy goat Gruff," said the second goat.

"Good," yelled the troll. "My tummy is grumbling for goat and you are going to be my lunch!"

"Wait," cried the goat in a deeper voice. "My bigger brother will be right along. I might be a small meal for you, but he'll make a delicious feast."

So the troll rumbled and grumbled, but he let the second goat pass over to the green pastures.

Moments later, the bridge went *TRIP-TRAP, TRIP-TRAP!*
It was so loud that for a moment the troll thought
it was thundering. He hated rain.

"Who's that tripping over my bridge!" roared the troll. "I've waited too long, and now I'm ready to fill my gullet with goat!"

"It is I, the biggest
billy goat Gruff. I've got long,
pointy horns to make Swiss cheese
of your body, and big, hard hooves to
mash your bones to bits!"

But the troll was too greedy to listen to what the big goat had to say. He licked his lips and said, "I'm going to gobble you up." Then he lumbered toward the big goat.

The biggest billy goat Gruff simply turned around and gave the troll a little . . .

KICK! . . .

. . . that sent him flying into the raging river below. The river carried the troll far, far away, and he was never heard from again.

As the sun went down, the big billy goat Gruff joined his smaller brothers in the meadow where the grass was so fresh and delicious they couldn't stop eating it. In fact, they got so fat, they could hardly walk home again.

So snip, snap, snout.
This tale's told out.